*With Courage
Resistance and
Love*

Courage is a Muscle

Soup

It's All About the Pathways

The Day We Stopped

Sorry to Trouble You

Old Blood and Young Teeth

Red

Sushi

The Letter

It Isn't Punk to Seek Permission

Christine

Sage

Pessimism is for Lightweights

Introduction

This work is dedicated to every person who is using their muscle, their voice, their platform, their work, their art, their time and energy to speak out and stand up for human rights. This work is for all the Nasty Women of the world! When a country elects a president, a prime minister and leadership that does not protect or speak up for the human rights of the people of that country, then we will be forced to unite and rise up to do the vital work of protecting ourselves, ourselves. So, here are thirteen pieces of courage and resistance, pieces inspired by protest, poems written for the women's march and for people on the front line, pushing for equality, for justice, for peace, for women's empowerment and amplification. Anti-hate poems. Poems dedicated to people trying to save the NHS, the doctors and nurses, the emergency services and the teachers. People fighting to save the libraries, the live music venues and pubs, the heart of our community and our humanity. This collection contains a letter from the spirit of Hope herself. I thank you, and share these efforts with love and with solidarity.

Courage is a Muscle

Courage is the muscle
we use when we speak,
if we're being talked over
and told we're too weak.

And when we get weary
and when it gets tough,
it's our united courage says
Enough is enough.

Courage is the muscle
we work night and day,
to get equal rights
to get equal pay.

Our blood is taxed
our blood is shame,
our courage unites us
for we all bleed the same.

Courage is the muscle
we flex when we must,
courage is the muscle
for truth and for trust.

Courage is the muscle
we use when we speak,
if we're being walked over
and told we're too weak.

And when we get weary
we march side by side,
100 years, we're still marching
with courage and with pride.

Soup

Imagine if seven people from seven nationalities
Came to your home to share one pot of soup,
You would have seven conflicting versions of that soup.

One would write to note the flavour. Another the heat.
Someone would write about the meaning of soup.
The size of the portions. The memory the soup triggers.
Too salty. Not enough meat.
This is a stew? It's more a casserole!
This soup is a meal in itself!
I'm gluten intolerant!

The hungriest person at the table might just write—
Thank you

This is human nature—
We look around the table and
Examine the world as we do these dinner guests.
We note our differences—
Skin and manners and clothes and language.

And we forget to sing!
We forget to celebrate that we are one,
That the act of love was sitting down together
And sharing the pot of soup in the first place.

We say nothing
As they put someone in prison
For using a fork to eat their soup.
We silence the person that slurps soup from the bowl.
We ignore all the women because…
What the hell does a woman know about soup anyway?
Some around the table demand bread with their soup,
Others feel entitled to the whole pot of soup, just for them.
There's one, there is always one, who will spit in the soup
So that the soup is ruined for everyone,
And sadly this is all human nature too.

I am too sad to finish this poem about soup
I'll just say I have so much to be grateful for
I'm so lucky I have a warm kitchen
I have a pot and some vegetables

Today I'll make time
Today I'll make love
Today I'll make soup
Don't make war
Make love and
Make soup.

It's All About the Pathways

K said
we make
neural pathways
in our head
for people
to process ideas
we make connections
and repetitions
K said
grief hurts and
losing someone hurts
and death is painful
because your head
is dissolving
the neural pathway
that was made
for that person
it grows in your head
K said
like a branch of ivy
in your head
K said
and it works the other way
for example
a racist has made a
neural pathway
of hate

a pattern of repetition
a narration of a version
of events
and the more
the racist repeats that story
the thicker that branch grows
when we latch
onto an idea like
loving someone
or like
hating someone
we make a pathway
sticking to one narration
one version about a person or subject
until the ivy knots in our head
K said
and the branch
gets thicker and thicker
the pathways
we create
love and hate
we get stuck
and we
cannot see
reason or light.

COU

RAGE

The Day We Stopped

There was hardly any resistance.

You'd think there would be more panic, more protests, more anger, more about it on the news. They pulled up in plain vans and marched into public spaces—the parks and the shopping centres in broad daylight, they read charges, arrested people, one by one.

I stared, we stared, we stood still and stared, as people were calmly selected and handcuffed and escorted away.

I was captured, but even I hardly resisted. You'd think that I would make more fuss, that I would be dragged, kicking and screaming. But I seem to recall apologising to them in their uniforms, with their masks and guns.

We were taken away. To a place just like here and now, but we were not free to leave. In the beginning we tried to run away, we plotted and planned how to escape but we were heavily guarded.

I remember we whispered in the dark, we said it was wrong, we wept and said we missed our lives our families, our lovers, our children.

I tried to escape once, I ran for it, got as far as some dreams, but a hand covered my mouth and I was taken down.

As time passed I grew to become a model prisoner. I learned how to be subservient, obedient and quiet. How strange it was when the singing stopped, that is what I am remembering most. The deafening silence. The whispering stopped, the nudge of notes stopped. Funny how this place was once all bite and scratch and graffiti, but one by one we stopped shouting and kicking and fighting and running away.

This place was inside and there was no outside to run to. This was normal as home. Our freedom was past, our past erased. Our history a burnt book. We were as sedate as bored lions in the zoo. We stopped asking questions and making demands, we ate whatever we were fed and did as we were told. And when it was dark, we slept dreamlessly. We stopped seeing the walls, because we stopped looking.

But now I am here. I stand in an empty space. Looking up at a still and grey sky, I am alone for the first time in a very long time. I am walking in an ordinary park. There's a damp chill in the air. Wet grass, crunch of dead leaves below my feet. A silence and stillness.

I'm not being followed, or chased or pursued by dogs, but I keep walking because I'm unsure if I have escaped or if I am still dreaming? If I am inside or outside, if I even existed? Can anyone see me? Will anyone read this? I don't know if I am sleepwalking.

I walk around the park perimeter and write this in my head. I keep walking inside the railings of the park in a circle. I memorise this, her voice inside me. It is a sad and strange poem, all of it is sad and strange. I did not write these words, but they spiral in my remembering. Over and over again, she is speaking, calling to me and she sounds like this:

the day we get lost is the day we stop dreaming is the day we stop longing is the day we stop fighting is the day they make us think we are free is the day we stop running is the day we forget is the day we remember is the day we stopped speaking is the day we forget the words is the day we stop reading is the day we stop writing is the day we stop praying and wishing and hoping is the day we stop loving is the day we stop living is the day we lose the colour and the light and the heat and the joy is the day we get lost is the day we are lost is the day we stop laughing is the day we believe we are free is the day we stop dreaming is the day we stop running is the day we stop fighting is the day we stop singing is the day we stopped singing is the day one by one we fall one by one we fall one by one we fall

Silent.

Sorry to Trouble You

They call them
the troubled poets
I love poets
who are troubled
poets causing trouble
and troubling other poets
poets troubled
by drunkenness and
nightmares and insomnia
troubled poets
troubled by depression
heart sick isolation
I love troubled poets
troubled by poverty and hunger
writing poetry by a tea light
with a stolen job centre pen
a spider for an audience
a cigarette for heat
drinking cooking lager
I love troubled poets
troubled by conflict
scribbling poems
in Yarl's Wood
Immigration Removal Centre
on their own wrist
with a piece of glass

I love troubled poets
troubled in refugee camps
troubled in children's homes
troubled in shop doorways
sleeping rough in rain soaked rags
relying on food banks
eating cold beans from the tin
using newspaper for a sanitary towel
troubled poets
troubled in the trenches
troubled by apathy
troubled by abuse and torture
poets writing in blood in prison cells and
given public lashings for writing
just for writing blogs and publishing poems and then
stoned to death in the town square for their trouble
troubled poets writing and fighting for human rights
troubling themselves with all that is unsaid
and all that is meant inside the graffiti
I love a poets troubled cry
thank fuck for that
bless you, you troubled poet
I thank you
for troubling yourself

I love you
troubled poets who start trouble
speaking up for freedom
for an end to the killing
I hear you troubled poets
troubled by silence, violence
troubled by lack of light, lack of truth
troubled by the troubles of the world
rocks in your pockets and
stones under the tongue
wading into icy water
tying a hangman noose around a troubled throat
gargling your troubled words to the end
I love troubled poets that trouble themselves
peeling onions in a Calais kitchen
protesting at Downing Street
Stormzy singing—
You think we forgot about Grenfell?
I love that, that troubled poet
troubled poets sharing, airing their troubles in public
poets who trouble themselves with trouble
I love the poets who are bothering to trouble us
poets who bother to trouble themselves
troubled poets who are troubled by this
this terrible, terribly troubling
troubled troubled world

Old Blood and Young Teeth

A life is so short
When you consider the age
Of the temples and cathedrals
Built with the faith and old blood of men
Who lived short lives and then died
In the name of their Gods and their God's immortality
Consider the age of that gold Buddha
It is older than the crippled tree
That was planted when it was erected
But younger than the river beneath it
And the ocean must be oldest of all
And the years of the sun and the moon?
Who is eldest? The sun or the moon?
And the age of fire, how old is fire?
How old is water? Is rain older than flame?
And the teeth in your head are so young, my love
The teeth in your head are so young
The teeth in your head are so young compared to your brain
What thoughts your brain had before your teeth grew
And your old heart, how faithfully it beats, old timer
Your ears listened and heard you scream
As that first tooth tore through
And the first thing
Your first tooth gnawed
Was your own finger

All of us, every one of us, had to grow teeth last
Every one of us had to grow our teeth last
So smile now, show me your young teeth
Smile and show us all your spring chicken tooth
Smile and let your first dream soar
Smile now and feel that love beat in your old chest
And shine out of those big old eyes of yours
Your shiny old eyes in your old bone skull head
But oldest of all is your old, old blood
Your blood is as old as time
And I love you
And I love every
drop.

Red

You should see what I made red
You should see what I made red
You should see my art
Look at my beetroot chutney
Look at me and my red soupy pants
You should see me now
On all fours groaning
Rocking back and forth
On my haunches
Breathing into it
Breathing out of it
Clinging to my hot water bottle like a life raft
Low frequency cramps
Punctuated by knitting needle cramps
With extra kick and prick
Like a scissors jab and snip inside my bloody hole
And the product is blackcurrant jelly, redcurrant syrup

You should see what I made red
You should see what I made red
You should see my art
The sheets, the sheets, the sheets
I made all the sheets red
All the bed a pool of red heat
In the bath there are floating globs

Chunky bloody marmalade
Black cherry vomit
Farmhouse strawberry jam
I'm having a very heavy time man!
But I won't make too much of a fuss
Just leave me here to bleed to death
The last thing we want is any fuss
Just leave me here to drown in my own blood
You should see what I make red
You should see what I made red
Real red and vivid as black cherry juice
Kidneys in my frying pants
My pyjamas are my butchers apron
I used a whole packet of pads in one day
Remarkable!

But if men had periods and I was a man I'd walk into a pub
Throw the empty packet down on the bar and yell—

Hey I am having the biggest one!
I used a whole packet in one day!

And I'd demand free drink, and the pub would all applaud
And the men would slap me on the back for having a big one
In the movie of this month
I would be played by Bruce Willis, Bleed Hard

But...
This blood does not come from violence
This blood does not come from murder
This blood is not my death
There are no bullets or knives
This is no wound or sickness
This blood is not a weakness
This blood is my moon, my time
This blood is all me

And yet this blood disgusts us the most
More than any blood
More than the blood on the hands of man's bloody war
This blood disgusts us most
This shameful blood, this quiet blood
Shush! Don't mention the lady blood
Shush! Don't mention this discreet blue lady blood

Yet we must pay tax for this silent blood
Every month we pay tax to bleed
This blood of ours is so very disgusting—
And so taxable.

And that tax goes to anti abortion charities
We are haemorrhaging women's rights
We are paying to bleed away a woman's choice
The tampon tax goes to battered women's charities

It's blood for blood,
Bleeding for bloody battered women
We are taxed to bleed to bleed to bleed to bleed.

So,
I'll get my money's worth
Come see what I paint red
You should see what I made red
Come see, come see what I made red
You should see my mess
The bathroom, the bedroom
Everything is stained with my stink
The whole world I paint it red, red, red
Come see, come see, come look

You should see what I made red
You should see me, see me,
See RED

Anything you can do I can do bleeding
I can do anything flooding with blood

Sushi

Do you remember the first time a man fed you sushi? It was a long time ago. Do you remember? He took you to the new Japanese restaurant. A bright and gladly lit place where the food goes around on a conveyor belt. Do you remember watching the food going around? Each plate of food assembled on rainbow plates just like the pictures on the wall. Do you remember the first bite? The first taste? The snap of pink ginger. The tuna was red as watermelon, but the texture, it was like his wet red tongue, but cold, raw, fish. Then the hard slap was wasabi, the sting, your nose tingling with blood. Do you remember the first time he hit you? Do you remember the first time you had sushi? The first time you were slapped? Do you remember the shock of the first time you were slapped by a man? Do you? Do you remember the heat? And the sushi? Your hot cheek. Stinging. Do you remember the pop of orange eggs? Do you remember the first time you had sushi? How strange is hot wine though, you said. Hot wine? It's not hot wine, he said. It is sake. Not wine. Sake. So embarrassed. Red cheeks. Do you remember? Do you remember you said sorry? Sorry. You said sorry the first time you were hit by a man. Remember how you apologised and how he cried, and you said sorry again. And he went very quiet and thundery and you felt guilty in his weather. Do you remember the guilt you felt the first time you made a grown man cry for hitting you? He cried. Do you remember making a grown man cry? Do you remember you did that? Remember the first time you saw a man in tears? How you'd never seen a man cry before, and you didn't know men cried like that, like girls, shaking shoulders, eyes all full up of sad and tears and, plop-plop-plop, tears weaving through his grown man bristles. His rough man cheeks all wet and it was your fault. You made him cry. You did this. He loves you so much. Sorry you said. Your cheek still hot. The inside of your arms bruised from him holding you and shaking you. Shaking you and shaking you like a wet dog. Shaking you blue. Blue bruises. Purple bruises. Green bruises. All colours down the inside of your arms. Bruises in fingerprints. You could see each fingerprint in the bruises where he held you tight and shook you and shook you. And it's your own fault. You're too wilful. You'll lose him if you aren't careful. Because he's ten years older than you, so he knows what real love is. And he paid for dinner and you had sushi and it's posh. And it's raw fish. And you didn't know sushi was raw fish because you're fifteen and he's twenty five and he knows things about the big wide world. And later he was all drink up, drink fast, eat this and eat that. Your mouth was stuffed full and you swallowed it all up to please him. You swallowed it all down to show him what a big girl you are. Do you remember that sashimi tuna tongue? Do you remember he hit you? Pulled and pushed you? Do you remember the first time a man hit you? The first time. The last time. The first time. The last time. Red. Raw. Sushi. Remember the first time. Remember the last time. Let that be the last time.

The Letter

Dear,
I hope you're well
I hope you're warm and dry
A safe place to lie your head
Some oranges, some fresh bread
I hope home is safe and sound
Shelter from a storm and high ground
I hope you make time to read and grow
And water all those seeds you sow
You know, you come, you know, you go
That is how the humans flow
Your geography is at best ambient
Temporary, transient
Clocks are maps, time is past
Nothing isn't meant to last
Fight or flight or run and flea
Not one of we can feel free
If some of we are locked in fear
That's how we've always been, my dear

My dear,
I post this in a letter
I hope, you can hold each other better
Wind and fire, fuel and wars
Weary feet cross desert floors
Broken boats and brutal sea and
Human greed and tyranny
Displacement, homeless, rearranging
Constant change is you, growing, changing

So,
I'll enclose a breath for healing
A match to burn all ill-feeling
A monarch butterfly wing
your migration is a magnificent thing
Here's some lint for all you built
A peppermint to suck and soothe your guilt
Your burning cities, your barren land
You drown with sharks, you choke on sand
Your lost babies, your bloody tissue
That you should bare that is the issue
Here's a bandage for your clots and splits
Your hurts and passing blames in it...
Where do we begin to bandage our world today?
Where's the root of all the pain?
Everything is blood stain
It's buried in your DNA
You carry tomorrow in yesterday
Human fox hunts human rights
Gnarling dogs snap in moonlight
Masts in harbour, ships on shore
Precious human cargo, stolen moor
Clocks are maps, time is fast
Everything is meant to pass
Fight or flight or run and flea
Not one of we can be free
If some of we are locked in fear
That's how we've always been, my dear

My dear,
I Hope you're well,
I Hope you're warm and dry
A safe place to lie your head
Some oranges, some fresh bread
Clean water and clean air
Space to grow, room to share
Home is just a marble in the sky
I roll it blue and green and I
Hope I am and Hope am I
See all that free sky up above
Live with Hope
Live with love,
With love,
Hope

It Isn't Punk to Seek Permission

Because if we had just one hour in your sun
We'd show you how it's done
We'd show you how quickly things can turn around
Go on, give us one hour in your sun
And watch us bloom a field of colour
Look, look how our labours blossom
Look how we flourish with no sun, no heat or warmth
Because we know how to make love grow in the frost
In the hard dirt, in the winter underground
We make magic mushroom from shit
And spin gold from flakes of hard life
Our hunger is bears, our thirst we share
No boots, no armour, nothing but love drives this
And love is where this comes from and
Love is who this is for and love knows
We have nothing but each other to protect this
No gloves, bare hands, no certainties
And no money, no, never any money
So go on, I dare you, and I dare it
Give us a go on your sun and watch how we'd share it
Give us a paddle in your sunlight, a splash of shiny-shiny
One hour of the sun that is fixed on you and your privilege
For look how strong we are and how tall we can already stand
Without your sun, without your gold and
Without your permission.

RESIST

TANCE

Christine

His mother called me a good time girl
They all said I was just looking for a good time
I was a teenager
I thought looking for a good time was a good thing
And her son
He gave me a good time, alright
He called me darling
Much later they all called me prostitute
Forever and ever
How fast they all turned their backs
So quick to betray daughters to protect the good old boys.

Sage

The hot moon
has nudged us awake
called us come
bare foot and
naked hearted
stones circle the flame
we cut and burn a ringlet
for all the memory hair holds
of you and of then
slit a fish throat
metaphorically
open the sea and all the wet sky
and then let go
of all those gulped words
it is safe to cough them up now
your throat jammed with rage and
furry with unspoken things
remember how they shushed you
for you were being a girl
too loud they said and such messy hair
then when you grew beautiful
and strong you were all wrong
so laugh, belly laugh
your teeth all liquorice
your face is a festival

mud and ash, smoke and cider
daub their doll's house in clots
add salt for the truth of it
and pepper for the courage this always takes
every lifetime over and over again
you are the survivor of ideas that cannot burn
you are your own ghosts wildest dream
here's some sage
stick that in your bowl and smoke it
burn ear wax for all the listening they will not do
an eyelash for the lucky charms of you
prick your finger and write in blood:
I promise I will never ever shush
then roar
bold enough to wake your elders
pour oil on the fire and spit and crackle
as all your hurts uncurl
add water
she remembers everyone
every drop of every one of us
be seen for which drop you are
the truth of it shines in your tears
take a good slug of rum and
then swig another and feel the burn
look it in the terrible eye
the spirit walking in your veins
you won't bleed for much longer

the trouble of it leaves you
tie it with string
place them feelings
in the doll's house
lock it, nice and neat
and miniature
and watch it burn
hot and orange and true
you'll never shush or shrink
finish the bottle of rum
leave none for the dying stars
nothing for the postman
bloody moon
midsummer's furious beauty
in a world that never changes
so march forwards
I promise
I will never ever shush you
we hold hands
love shines brightest
just then
as the moon sets
since all this blood began
we never, ever
give up.

Pessimism is for Lightweights

Think of those that marched this road before
And those that will march here in years to come
The road in shadow and the road in the sun
The road before us and the road all done
History is watching us and what will we become

This road is all flags and milestones
Immigrant blood and sweat and tears
Built this city, built this country
Made this road last all these years

This road is made of protest
And those not permitted to vote
And those that are still fighting to speak
With a boot stamping on their throat

There is power and strength in optimism
To have faith and to stay true to you
Because if you can look in the mirror
And have belief and promise you
Will share wonder in living things
Beauty, dreams, books and art
Love your neighbour and be kind
And have an open heart

Then you're already winning at living
You speak up, you show up and stand tall
It's silence that is complicit
It's apathy that hurts us all

Pessimism is for lightweights
There is no straight white line
It's the bumps and curves and obstacles
That make this road yours and mine

Pessimism is for lightweights
This road was never easy and straight
And living is all about living alive and lively
And love will conquer hate.

HOPE